ANNELIE
IN THE DEPTHS OF THE NIGHT

ANNELIE
IN THE DEPTHS
OF THE NIGHT

by Imme Dros

with drawings by Margriet Heymans
translated by Arno and Erica Pomerans

faber and faber
LONDON · BOSTON

First published in Great Britain in 1991
by Faber and Faber Limited
3 Queen Square London WC1N 3AU
This paperback edition first published in 1995

Photoset by Parker Typesetting Service, Leicester
Printed in England by Clays Ltd, St Ives plc

A CIP record of this book is available from the British Library

ISBN 0571 17351 9

10 9 8 7 6 5 4 3 2 1

Chapter 1

Grandma sings songs.

They are strange songs from the days when Grandma used to be a little girl. Strange to think that Grandma used to be a little girl.

She sings her songs in the kitchen, on the attic stairs, in the garden and on the lavatory. Annelie can't help but listen to them.

Sometimes the songs are familiar. 'Goosey, Goosey Gander'. 'Row, Row, Row Your Boat'. 'I Saw Three Ships Come Sailing By'.

Annelie joins in those songs. But most of the time they are strange songs.

> Softly strikes the evening-bell,
> All the world now comes to rest,
> Birds are singing mournful songs,
> The sun is sinking in the west.

That's a horrid song with a gloomy ending and Annelie puts her fingers in her ears whenever

1

Grandma sings it. Just as she does with 'By the Wall
of the Old Churchyard'. And with 'A Garland of
Flowers in Her Golden Hair'. And with 'Mummy,
Give Me a Little Horse'. Those are horrid, horrid
songs.

'Please sing something else, Grandma!'

'Very well, child.'

And Grandma sings something else.

> Hankypanky sits under the bridge,
> Selling logs of wood.
> Roll up, roll up, come and see,
> When you do you'll all agree,
> Hankypanky's wood's no good!

Annelie beats time with a tin soldier. The soldiers
are almost as old as Grandma. They used to come
with packets of tea. Given away free.

'Grandma, who is Hankypanky?'

'What's that, child? How about some hot
chocolate?'

Grandma often doesn't answer when you ask her
things. Or else she gives you an answer that is no
use at all.

2

'When will Daddy and Mummy be coming?'

'Oh, child, they may be quite a while.'

'How long is quite a while?'

'Go bring me some clothes-pegs, child. The basket is in the kitchen.'

Quite a while is taking a long time. Annelie has been staying with Grandma for some time already, four Sundays and all the days in between. Annelie keeps asking how soon Daddy and Mummy will be coming to fetch her, especially when it's time to go to bed at the top of the stairs.

Daddy had brought her without any warning one day, in his green car full to bursting with toys and clothes, not just summer things but pullovers for the winter too, and it isn't anything like winter yet. 'You'll be staying with Grandma for a little while.'

'How long is that?'

Daddy didn't say. Daddy often doesn't answer either when you ask him things, or else he gives you an answer that is no use at all.

'But where is Mummy?'

'She's going to be busy for quite a while.'

Quite a while.

'When will you be coming back, Daddy?'

'We'll have to see.' And Daddy had driven off without her.

Now she has to live at Grandma's and sleep at Grandma's in the little room at the front of the house, where Mummy used to sleep when she was a little girl, how strange that Mummy used to be a little girl.

It's a lovely room and you can see the sea from the window.

There is a round table with a little dark green china tea set, which Grandma lets you use for drinking real tea. There is a shaded lamp to daydream by and a reading lamp to look at pictures by. There is an armchair that rocks, with a cushion so plump that it fills the whole chair. There is a blue silk folding screen full of stars and moons, and there is a bookcase. There is a chest with clothes for dressing up and hats and fans and pieces of lace. There is a wall cupboard for Annelie's toys and for the toys Grandma and Mummy had when they were little girls.

And there is a bed, the most beautiful bed in the

4

world, with golden bars and a canopy with curtains hanging from it covered with the same little flowers as the eiderdown and the pillow slips. 'A bed fit for a princess,' says Grandma. Even so, Annelie doesn't really like sleeping in it, she would sooner have her own little bed, back home.

'When are Daddy and Mummy coming, Grandma?'

'You just have a good sleep, then soon it'll be tomorrow and tomorrow will make it one day less.'

'But how many days will still be left then?'

Grandma tucks the eiderdown in and sings one of her songs.

> Annelie must go to sleep,
> Or else the plants upstairs will creep,
> Dragon Tree and Tiger's Jaws.

'Not that song, Grandma!'

Grandma stops singing and goes downstairs. The stairs creak.

Annelie is all alone. She can hear sounds in the house and sounds outside. Birds on the roof, the wind in the trees. She can see the moon through the

window. Is the moon coming closer?

'Grandma!'

'What is it, child?'

'There's a scary noise, Grandma.'

'It's nothing to worry about. Just turtledoves. Go to sleep now!'

'Cinderella's doves?'

'Yes, doves like those. Good night.'

Cinderella's doves, from the picture in the kitchen above the cooker. That picture is even older than the tea soldiers, you can tell from its brown spots.

'It's got fox-marks,' says Grandma.

'And your hands have got fox-marks, too, Grandma, haven't they?'

'I call those my churchyard flowers,' says Grandma.

When Annelie is in the kitchen with Grandma she always has a good look at the picture with the fox-marks. Cinderella's feet are bare and she is dressed in a torn skirt. She has a small bowl of peas in her hand and there are white doves perched on her shoulders. Annelie stares at the picture for so long that sometimes it feels as if she is in there with Cinderella, in that strange house with the cinders

6

and the peas all over the floor. And now, lying in
bed, thinking about Cinderella, suddenly there she
is, inside that strange house.

'Grandma! Come and get me out!'

Occasionally Grandma can be a little bit cross.
Especially when she has already gone to bed herself
in the room at the back of the house.

'Child, whatever is it, waking me up in the depths
of the night?'

'Where's that? Where's the depths of the night?'

'Ssssh.'

'Is it deep like a foxhole?'

'Ssssh.'

'In the woods once I saw a foxhole and Daddy
said . . .'

'Ssssh.'

'It had fifteen passages and was at least a hundred
years old. Is that quite a while? A hundred years?'

Grandma starts singing again about the Dragon
Tree and the Tiger's Jaws.

'I'm asleep, I'm asleep.'

'See you in the morning, then, child.'

Annelie stares into the darkness. Everywhere is

dark. The depths of the night must be terribly deep, much deeper even than an ordinary foxhole. And it must have more than fifteen passages. But where can it be? In Grandma's bedroom? In the kitchen, behind the cooker? In the dyke in front of the house? Or behind the dyke, next to the sea? And are the passages made of sand or of something else?

She twists and turns. The pillow is lumpy, it's a horrid pillow. She kicks the blankets off, her foot hits one of the bars, they are horrid bars. The bed is too hard, and the bed is too soft.

When will Daddy and Mummy be coming to fetch her?

She shivers and ducks back under the eiderdown.

And then she sees the depths of the night.

Chapter 2

The depths of the night is lying quite casually under the eiderdown.

'You see?' thinks Annelie. 'It looks exactly like that foxhole. I thought as much. But it's much bigger and the walls aren't made of sand. No, it certainly isn't sand. But what is it?'

She crawls inside. The walls and the floor of the depths of the night are quite soft, as soft as down, softer than down . . . When Annelie pushes against one of the soft walls she can no longer see her own hand. And she can feel herself sinking into the floor. Where are her knees? Her feet? Where has everything gone?

'It's clouds!' cries Annelie. 'Lots and lots of clouds.' She lets herself fall over forward, and rolls about from side to side. 'Clouds. Real clouds. You see, you can sit on a cloud!'

She jumps up again and dances around, bouncing just as she used to bounce on the blow-up cushions

at the recreation ground. Clouds. Real clouds. At last she knows what it's like to walk on clouds. She had always thought it must be wonderful: walking on clouds. Daddy had said you couldn't do it, but Daddy obviously doesn't know everything.

She dances and she runs and she jumps further and further into the depths of the night, deeper and deeper.

Clouds, real clouds and changing all the time. Thin, streaky clouds, plump, fleecy clouds, thick thunderclouds, pink morning clouds, purple evening clouds.

Further she goes, and deeper and deeper.

Who would be living in the depths of the night? A snow fox? A red fox? A cloud fox perhaps with little cloud fox cubs? What do they eat? Clouds?

Further, further, further.

Cirrus clouds, cumulus clouds, rain clouds.

Further.

Just when she is beginning to get tired of it, she comes to the end of the passage. She can't be in the very depths of the night, because she is standing by a way out and beyond that it is blue. A golden boat

is lying there on a sea which has no dyke along it.

'Ahoy there!' calls the golden boat.

It is the Moon himself and he is waving to her.

'Are you coming along? Come on.'

Annelie climbs on board.

'Where to? Where shall we go?' asks the Moon, hoisting his sail.

'Let's go everywhere!' cries Annelie.

'That's the best plan,' says the Moon. He blows into the sail. They set off across the blue sea.

Chapter 3

The wind is rising and the Moon stops blowing.
They are sailing southwards.

Annelie looks over the side of the boat. Deep
down at the bottom of the sea are other seas, and
countries with mountains and forests. And rivers.
And a town. And another town. And the town
where Annelie lives. And the little square in front of
the school. And the house where Annelie lives.

'Fasten your seat-belts, we're about to land,' calls
the Moon.

They are gliding straight down towards the attic
window.

'You may now disembark, do not forget your
luggage, and please leave nothing behind in the
cabin,' says the Moon in a stewardess's voice.

'That's our back attic!' says Annelie.

'As if I didn't know,' says the Moon. 'Who looks
inside it more often, you or I?' He throws the anchor
out onto the flat roof.

12

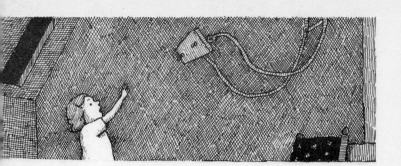

Annelie slips inside through the skylight. She is home. But the house is so quiet you could hear a pin drop. Only the swing is making a noise. It is squeaking in its rings, swinging all by itself. Does it do that every night? And it is singing as it swings:

> Yeeeow, yeeeow,
> Wood and rope,
> Annelie's home, for good, we hope.
> Yeeeow, yeeeow,
> Rope and wood,
> Annelie's naughty, Annelie's good.

When it gets to the end it screeches loudly.
'Aha! Are you there?'
'No, I'm here.'
'That's what I said.'
'No, that's not what you said, you said . . .'
'I know what I say and I knew what I said and what you say is what you are,' screeches the Swing, and starts to sway about wildly, higher and higher.
'Not so high, not so high,' cries Annelie. She is frightened. Any minute now the Swing will fly out of its hooks and hit someone on the head.

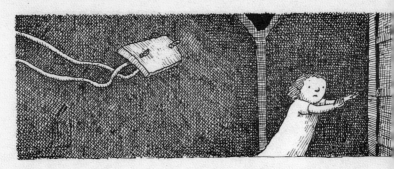

The Swing swoops up and down. 'Yeeeow, yeeeow, ooooeee, ooooeee.'

The Moon is nowhere to be seen and the house is certainly empty. It is much too quiet. Daddy and Mummy aren't here. They have gone. Four Sundays and all the days in between.

'Yeeeow, yeeeow, yeeeow!'

'Oh, my goodness, Swing, not so high, please, don't go so hi-i-i-i-igh!'

The Swing doesn't listen.

Annelie creeps behind the laundry basket, but the Swing knows where she's gone and makes straight for her.

'Go away, go away!' sobs Annelie.

'You'd like that, wouldn't you, you nasty little girl, you naughty little girl, naughty Annelie, yeeeow, yeeeow.'

There is only one way out. Annelie flees towards the Mousebox.

Chapter 4

She is so horribly frightened of the Swing that she goes right inside the Mousebox. She would never dare to otherwise.

Because the Mousebox is a creepy place. Dark and strange, with rustles and squeaks in every nook and cranny. There are mice inside it, and that's how the boxroom got its name: Mousebox. But it has a Sunday name, too. On Sundays the boxroom is called the Darkroom, and Daddy goes inside to print all the photographs he has taken. Of Mummy and Annelie by the foxhole in the dunes. And of them by the sea, with little boats on the water. And by the little white house next to the dyke where Grandma lives, and by the green car.

And every so often the boxroom is given another nickname. Sometimes it is called the Junk Room. And there is a lot of junk in it, that's true. More than in the shed or in the attic. Too much junk, Mummy says. But Daddy won't ever throw anything out.

15

There are boxes and bags and chests and cases.
Pots and pans and bins and kettles and vases. All of
them have something just a little bit wrong with
them. And then there are the bottles. Annelie isn't
ever allowed to touch the bottles. She isn't allowed
to open them and she certainly isn't allowed to drink
out of them.

'The stuff in those bottles has a nasty bite,' Daddy
must have said at least a hundred times.

Well, anybody can see that. The bottles have
sharp little teeth in their mouths. They growl softly
and click their little molars together. Clickety-click.
They snap at Annelie's legs and try to grab hold of
her.

'No, no!' shouts Annelie and jumps away to one
side, past the piles of sheet music and the mountain
of shoes. She stumbles over the shoelaces coiled all
over the floor, as thick as the roots of trees.

And then, by pure chance, she spots Mummy's
wedding shoes. The most beautiful shoes in the
world. Made of white satin. It's called satin when it
gleams so softly and feels so smooth under your
fingers.

16

Annelie puts the shoes on. Mummy doesn't mind, she lets her put the satin shoes on now and then and walk about in them. With them on, Annelie feels brave enough to go back to the attic. The heels are so high that the bottles can't do anything to her any more.

'And where d'you think you're off to?' says a voice from behind the skates.

Annelie gets such a fright that she falls over the sledge.

She is not alone in the boxroom. A perfect stranger is there as well, a woman who is wearing at least ten frocks, one on top of the other: summer frocks over thick woollen winter frocks, frocks with little dots over frocks with stripes or frocks with checks, frocks with lace, and frocks with feathers and fur over beach frocks.

'Give me those shoes, girl,' says the Frock Woman. She is smiling a sugary-sweet smile but she has long eye-teeth. 'Give them to me, hand them over.'

'No,' says Annelie, 'they're Mummy's and I'm allowed to wear them. They aren't yours.'

'Give,' says the woman even more softly and
sweetly, 'givegivegivegive. Gimmegimme-
gimmegimme. Give me those satin shoes, give me
those shiny, slippery, shimmery, satiny wedding
shoes. Mine! Mine! Mineymineymineymine.'

She smiles still more softly and sweetly. Her eye-
teeth flash, her fingers have ten long, curved nails.

Annelie screams out loud, 'Help!'

'I beg your pardon?' says a sharp little voice quite
near by. 'What do you mean, help?'

'Help. The Frock Woman is after me.'

'Oh, I see. Well, you'd better come over here then,
Nitwit,' says the sharp little voice. 'Imagine walking
about in such fancy shoes for all to see. This way!'

A slender paw beckons from a mousehole.

Annelie gets down on the floor and wriggles
through the small opening. She can just about
manage to squeeze through, but the Frock Woman is
too fat.

She gets stuck fast and calls out in a wheedling
voice: 'Isn't there a hole somewhere that a real lady
can go through?'

'What's she saying?' whispers Annelie, hoarse

18

with fright. 'She doesn't mean well, I'm sure of that.'

'Pay her no heed,' says the mouse with the sharp little voice. He looks like an ordinary house mouse except that he has a red moustache. 'Now, can I get you anything?'

'I am rather thirsty,' says Annelie.

The mouse with the red moustache pulls open a large cupboard and points to a lot of glasses full of fruit squash. 'What flavour do you like best?'

'Oh, raspberry. I like that best of all.'

He hands her a glass of red-coloured squash. But when she has drunk it all up she still feels thirsty. The mouse gives her a fresh glass as often as she wants. Yellow squash, orange squash, green squash, purple squash. The empty glasses rattle together on the mousetable.

'So thirsty,' moans Annelie, 'so terribly thirsty.'

'Here's some water,' says the mouse. 'Have a drink, child, whatever is the matter?'

The mouse is Grandma. She is standing beside the bed with a mug in her hand. It is light in the room. It is daytime.

19

Chapter 5

'Are there any mice with red moustaches, Grandma?'

'No, child, I shouldn't have thought so.'

'There was one in the Mousebox.'

'Oh, in the Mousebox,' says Grandma.

'What are you knitting?'

'A thick pullover for the winter.'

'But it isn't winter yet, is it?'

'Not yet, but it will be in a little while.'

You can't argue with that.

'Are we going out shopping soon, Grandma?'

Shopping is fun, at any rate. Grandma carries a large shopping bag and Annelie a small one. She is given something nice in every shop. A slice of sausage, a sweet, an apple. The shops are along the dyke, just like Grandma's house.

'When it's winter and there's snow you'll be able to slide down the dyke on a sledge,' says Grandma.

'But by the time it's winter I'll have been back home for ages.'

'And there is the school,' says Grandma, paying no attention to Annelie. 'See what a big playground there is?'

'Our playground is miles bigger,' says Annelie.

'Will you give me a hand with the cooking, child?'

Grandma is a wonderful cook and she's teaching Annelie. Did the wings of Cinderella's doves move just then?

'What are you standing about dreaming for, child? Are you tired?'

No, she isn't tired, but she wants to go to bed all the same.

'Grandma, I know where to find the depths of the night.'

'That's good, child,' says Grandma. 'Sweet dreams.'

The Moon is shining through Annelie's window. He is fatter than he was last night.

'Hello, Moon,' says Annelie.

It feels lovely and warm under the eiderdown. Will the depths of the night still be there? Or has it vanished like the little mirror with the clown on the back? Vanished for no good reason, never to be found again?

'Pullovers for the winter. Lovely pullovers for the winter. Warm, woolly, winter pullovers.'

'But it isn't winter yet,' says Annelie.

A hedgehog is standing beside the entrance to the depths of the night. His back is full of spines, knitting needles like the ones Grandma keeps in her knitting bag.

'No pullover, then?' asks the hedgehog. 'In that case would you care to hire a sledge? The sledge is given away free with packets of tea, but the poles will cost you a kiss.'

He pulls two Number Seven knitting needles out of his back and holds out a grey cheek to Annelie.

The kiss has a nasty taste and the cheek prickles, just like Uncle Henk's.

'Gee-up, off you go!' calls the hedgehog.

The sledge slides smoothly through the passage in the clouds. Annelie pushes herself along smartly with the poles.

'So there you are,' says a familiar, sharp little voice next to her.

It's the mouse with the red moustache, on skates. 'You are that silly child with the satin shoes, aren't you?'

'Where are my shoes?' asks Annelie. 'What have you done with them?'

'They're under the table in my little house. Stands to reason. Come with me.'

The mouse turns down a side passage and they arrive at a round door. He knocks and calls out: 'Is anyone at home?'

'No, nobody's at home,' he calls back to himself.

'We can go in,' he says to Annelie, 'nobody's at home. The satin shoes are right there, under the mousetable.'

'Has the Frock Woman gone?' asks Annelie.

'You never can tell,' says the mouse, 'and even if she has, there's still a good chance that the Dragon Tree and the Tiger's Jaws will be creeping about. It was a bit stupid of you to go into that boxroom.'

'I didn't know there was a Frock Woman inside,' says Annelie.

'You would have done better to have stayed out of my room altogether,' says the mouse.

'It isn't your room, it's our Junk Room.'

'My name is Darkroom!' bawls the boxroom.

'There you go, now you've hurt his feelings.'

'Can a boxroom talk?' asks Annelie.

'Can't a boxroom talk from time to time?'

'I don't know.'

'You could fill a whole book with what you don't know, Numbskull.'

'If you can't be polite to me, I'd rather go,' says Annelie. 'You're just a tiresome mouse with a red moustache.'

'No!' The mouse clutches his snout. 'Not a red moustache! You don't mean red!'

'Yes. Red.'

'Really red? Not by any chance salmon-pink, or lilac, or purple?'

'Red, red, red.'

'Well, that's it, then, I might just as well call it a day,' says the mouse and starts to cry. 'Red! It couldn't be worse. I might as well give up altogether.'

'Give what up?'

'Everything,' sobs the mouse. 'Everything I ever hoped for, everything I lived for, everything I longed for and that my heart desired.'

'Just because your moustache is red?'

24

'Of course because of that, Nincompoop! You really haven't any idea, have you? A red moustache is the worst of all the bad things that can happen to a mouse. And there are plenty of bad things, believe me. The Dragon Tree and the Tiger's Jaws, the cat, the bat, the vampire. They're all horribly bad, but they're nothing compared with a red moustache. A red moustache is worse than no moustache at all.'

'I didn't know that.'

'You could fill a whole book with what you don't know, Noodlemug.'

'If you go on calling me names I shan't help you.'

'You, help me? Me, a mouse with a red moustache? No one can help me. Oh dear, oh dear, oh dear. A red moustache.'

'I could paint it,' says Annelie. 'There's some paint in our Mousebox.'

'My name is Darkroom!' roars the boxroom.

'You've hurt his feelings again, but never mind, what were you saying? Paint? Not green paint, by any chance, perhaps, mayhap, maybe?'

'Green paint for our fence.'

'Could you really fix me up with a green moustache?'

'If you want.'

'If I want? What mouse wouldn't? He who has a green moustache is king. Mouseking!'

'And is that what you want? To be Mouseking?'

'Who wouldn't want to be Mouseking!'

'I wouldn't!'

'Ha, ha, ha, you couldn't be even if you tried. You're too bald, you've got no fur and no moustache. You wouldn't have a hope.'

'I could paint your moustache but I'm too frightened to go back into the Junk Ro . . .'

'Watch it! I shan't tell you again!' bellows the boxroom.

'I'm too frightened to go back into the Darkroom.'

'That's more like it,' says the boxroom, 'and it's quite safe for you to come inside. The Frock Woman has gone. She's sitting on the Swing.'

Annelie goes and looks about inside the Darkroom, and comes back with two tins of green paint. Dark green and light green.

The mouse is speechless with happiness. He allows himself to be painted by Annelie. Dark green on the left and light green on the right.

26

'Now I am King,' he says.

Annelie curtseys to him.

'Make way, everybody, out of the way. I am the King,' cries the Mouse with the Painted Moustache.

'But there's nobody here,' says Annelie.

'That's what you think,' says the King.

Chapter 6

Mice who weren't there before are popping up all over the place.

'King? What King? Which King?' they squeak.

'Make way, make way, subjects.'

'See that? He's got a green moustache.'

'He's a King.'

'Of course he's a King, his moustache is green.'

'Hurrah!'

'Where did this King suddenly come from then?'

The mice whisper and bow.

The Mouse with the Painted Moustache walks majestically into the Darkroom past the Skate Mountain, the Sledge, the Shoe Mountain and the Sheet Music Pile.

Annelie carries his tail.

'Make way, make way for the King and his Tailbearer.'

They are all enjoying the solemn moment when

suddenly they can hear the squeaking of the Swing
and the laughter of the Frock Woman.

'Higher, higher, more, more!' the Frock Woman is
shrieking.

'Careful! Keep to the sides,' whispers the King.

Hugging the skirting board, they edge towards
the skylight, where a golden rope ladder hangs
down to the floor.

'See, I'm expected,' says the King. 'A golden
ladder for the King.'

But Annelie knows that the ladder is there for her,
and that the Moon is waiting outside.

They climb and climb. There are a hundred golden
rungs. On the window-sill they stop to take a rest
and immediately the Frock Woman spots the
shimmer of the white shoes in the moonlight.

'There's that child with my shoes, quick, get over
to that side!' she shouts to the Swing.

Annelie and the King jump out of the window.

It's just as well that the Moon has turned his sail
into a safety net.

'So you're here at last,' grumbles the Moon.

'May the King come along, too?' asks Annelie.

'A King may always come along,' says the King.

The Moon grumbles a bit more.

'I can't take every King who wants to come along.'

'Come on, now, dear Moon.'

'Oh, all right, then, let the Mouse come along. If you sing me a song, that is.'

All this talking has taken time and the Frock Woman is coming alarmingly close to the skylight. The Swing is continuing to pay out its ropes. They seem to be endless.

'Look out! The Frock Woman!' cries Annelie.

The Moon pulls the anchor free and off they go. Just in time, for the Swing comes flying out through the skylight and chases after the Moon on ropes that are getting longer and longer.

The Frock Woman shrieks after them: 'I'll catch you yet, you'll see, I'll catch you yet!'

'What an uncouth person,' says the Moon. 'Common as muck, nothing but riffraff. Come on, then, let's have some singing. You first and the Mouse next. Then we shan't be able to hear the Frock Woman.'

Annelie knows one of Grandma's songs about the Moon.

The Moon is peeping, the Moon is peeking,
Through the windowpane,
To see if the children are tucked up in bed,
Or still playing outside in the lane.

'Now that is a splendid song, and absolutely spot-on,' says the Moon, gratified. 'And now it's the Mouse's turn. Come on, Mouse! Sing!'

It seems that the Mouse with the Green Moustache is only too happy to oblige. He stands up with his paws on his heart and throws out his chest. His voice is suddenly deep and full of emotion, and he draws out each note for a long time as he sings:

Gondola, gondola, the Moon's golden shell,
Bring back from afar my princess safe and well,
Green my moustache, my heart rent in twain,
Without my princess I shall die of the pain.

'That's a splendid song, too,' says the Moon, 'splendid.'

'I didn't know you could sing,' says Annelie.

'Every king can sing,' says the Mouse with the Green Moustache, 'ask anybody.'

He sings a few more songs.

Far away in the distance they can see the Frock Woman on the Swing, small as a pinhead.

'We're there,' says the Moon.

Chapter 7

'We're there, and in splendidly good time, too,' says
the Moon.

'For what?' asks Annelie.

'For everything, of course,' says the Moon,
'because we can go left or we can go right, or we can
go forwards or we can go backwards. Or what have
you.'

'Wrong!' cries the King. 'We can go only one way,
one way at a time.'

The Moon and the King start to shout at each
other.

'Stop it, Moon, stop it, King!'

The Moon and the King shout even harder than
before.

''Tis, 'tis, 'tis! It's true, because if you're going one
way and you decide to turn back then backwards
suddenly becomes forwards, so there are many
more ways than forwards or backwards or to the left
or to the right.'

'Tisn't, 'tisn't, 'tisn't! There's only one way to go at a time, it doesn't matter how long you take to think about it and pick it out, and weigh up the pros and cons, there's only one way at a time.'

'There are heaps of ways!'

'There's only one way!'

'There are as many ways as there are stars in the sky!'

'There's one way and one way only!'

'Stop it, stop quarrelling so much!' cries Annelie.

'Craters to you!' cries the Mouseking.

'Rats to you!' cries the Moon.

'That's an insult!' yells the Mouseking.

'Serves you right!' roars the Moon.

Annelie starts to cry.

'Look what you've done now. You've made her cry.'

'No, I didn't. You did!'

'It was you!'

'It was you!'

'Stop it, stop it,' sobs Annelie. 'Why do you have to quarrel so much? Quarrelling all the time and I haven't the faintest idea what it's all about.'

34

The Moon and the King look at each other out of the corners of their eyes.

'I'm sorry, Moon.'

'I didn't mean it, King.'

'Just tell us where to go, Annelie.'

Annelie doesn't know. She doesn't know many places. 'Our house . . . Grandma's house . . . the school . . . the recreation ground . . . the swimming baths.'

'That's a lot,' says the Moon, 'because once you know one house, you know them all, and once you know one school, you know them all. And who peeps through all the windows? Me.'

'And once you know the way from your home to school then you know every way. Every way goes somewhere and comes from somewhere. That's all,' says the King.

'And if you can swim you won't drown and a lamppost is made of iron,' the Moon says scornfully.

'You can drown even if you can swim.'

'Oh, yes,' says the Moon. 'You can get cramp or you can get caught in the current.'

'Or you can end up going west,' says the Mouseking.

'Which west?' asks the Moon. 'North-west perhaps?'

'Any west. What are you drivelling about? You don't know any of them, anyway.'

'Me? Not know the points of the compass? Don't make me laugh. I know all thirty-two of them! And anyone who knows those can never get lost.'

'Swank, swank, swank. Empty words from a full moon.'

Then the Moon starts to gabble and the Mouseking gabbles even louder at the same time to put him off.

'North! North by east! North-north-east! North-east by north! North-east! North-east by east! East-north-east! East by north! East!'

'For goodness' sake stop it, you're making my head hurt!' cries Annelie.

But the Moon and the Mouseking keep on shouting.

'East by south! East-south-east! South-east by east! South-east! South-east by south! South-south-east! South by east! South!'

'Stop it! Stop it! It hurts!'

'South by west. South-south-west! South-west by south! South-west . . . Hey, what's the matter with Annelie?'

'It's your fault, Moon.'

'It's your fault, Mouseking.'

'Annelie, dear Annelie, aren't you well?'

'It's my head, it hurts so. Every time you shout, it makes my head hurt.'

'We're sorry,' mumbles the Moon.

'The two of you keep shouting at each other and I haven't the faintest idea what it's all about. Why don't you just talk normally?'

'We're too old for that,' says the Moon. 'I'm as old as the world, you know.'

'And I'm as old as my tail.'

'Yes, you're both old,' says Annelie. 'You're both too old for me.'

'Come now, we aren't as old as all that,' says the Moon. 'You're only as old as you feel!'

'I can still jump over a cat, you wait and see,' boasts the Mouseking.

'You're both old, old, old!'

'Aren't you a horrid little girl!'

'Little girls have to be nice, you know, otherwise they get thrown out on their ear.'

'Why should I be nice when the two of you are both so nasty to each other?'

'I don't know why exactly, that's just the way it is,' says the Moon.

'You'll get a good hiding otherwise, that's why,' says the Mouseking.

'But when I'm grown up I'll hit you back,' says Annelie. 'I'll remember every slap and I'll give them all back. When I'm grown up.'

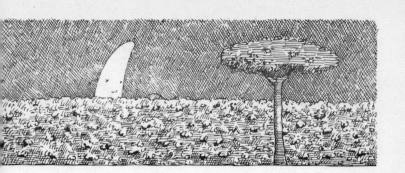

Chapter 8

They've been walking for quite some time along a
narrow path through meadowland. There is a hedge
on their right-hand side. The bushes are green with
blue patches of shade, just like on Uncle Nick's
paintings. It is growing dark. The land in the
distance looks unfamiliar.

'There's a circus on the other side of this hedge,'
says the Moon.

'How do you know that?' asks the Mouseking.
'You're just making it up.'

'I can look over the hedge.'

'Oh, so you can. And what's more, you're right,'
says the King.

'And how do you know that?' asks the Moon.

'I can look under the hedge.'

'A circus! That's where I want to go,' cries
Annelie. 'You said I could choose.'

They walk all the way round the hedge and find
themselves in a farmyard. The farmhouse and the

stables are dark, no light can be seen. A large tent
has been put up in a meadow, and there are three
rows of caravans painted in many different colours.

'I can hear the rustling of straw,' whispers the
Mouseking. 'There wouldn't be any cats round here,
would there?'

'I can hear the creaking of ropes and the flapping
of sails,' mutters the Moon.

'I can hear sighing,' says Annelie.

They listen to the sighs. There are snoring sighs,
squeaking sighs, groaning sighs, giggling sighs,
growling sighs, sobbing sighs, hard and soft sighs,
long and short sighs, just plain sighs and sighs you
can hardly hear. And the rustling in the straw
certainly does not come just from cats, if there are
any cats. Bodies both large and small are shifting
and fidgeting about in the straw, here a
heavyweight tossing and turning, there a paw
moving, or a tail, and very close to them the straw is
crackling as if someone were crying and trying not
to make a sound.

When they step into the tent the noise becomes
almost deafening. There is a storm of rustling,

creaking, squeaking and blowing.

'What is going on here?' asks Annelie.

'Sleeping is what's going on here,' says the Moon.

'Does everyone make noises when they sleep?' asks Annelie.

'You can say that again,' says the King. 'You've got to stay awake if you want to keep as quiet as a mouse.'

'Why are all the animals kept in cages?' asks Annelie.

'It's always like that at the circus,' says the Moon. 'Always has been.'

Annelie stands still.

'I thought I liked circuses,' she says, 'but this place is really horrid.'

'The performance hasn't started yet, and you can't tell without a performance. Just you wait for the glitter and the bright lights and the ice creams in the interval. A circus is marvellous, you'll see.'

They don't have long to wait. Suddenly all the lights go on and a fat man shouts through a horn: 'The performance is about to start, the performance is starting.'

'How can that be?' asks Annelie. 'Everybody's asleep.'

'That was in your dream,' says the fat man.

He points towards the cages, but there are no more cages to be seen, red velvet curtains with golden tassels are hanging there instead. Through a gap between the curtains the artistes and the animals now enter in a colourful procession.

'Three cheers for the circus,' cries the fat man. 'There's nothing to beat a circus. Music! Music!'

'The music is much too loud,' complains Annelie, 'and I know for a fact that there are cages behind those curtains.'

'Hold your tongue and clap your hands. Where are your manners?' hisses the fat man. 'Do I have to remind you that you're not at home?'

It's a funny sort of performance because all the animals and all the artistes appear at the same time. High up in the roof trapeze artistes fly towards each other and then away from each other, down below horses trot about, a bear rides on a child's bicycle, monkeys form a pyramid, a juggler and a conjurer snatch balls and little flags from each other.

42

Annelie hardly knows what to look at next.

Then the clown appears. The clown from the little
mirror that vanished. He bows specially to Annelie
and doffs his hat to her with a flourish, and then
because there is another hat under that hat he doffs
that one to her as well, but under the second hat
there is another hat and under that hat there is a
very large hat with feathers and under that there is a
fur cap and under that a helmet and under that a
bowler and under that an enormous sombrero and
under that . . .

'Stop!' shouts Annelie. She is getting quite dizzy,
and her head is throbbing.

The clown laughs and with lightning speed puts
the whole pile of hats back on his head. But then
suddenly he plucks a spotted bow-tie out from
under his chin.

'No!' protests Annelie.

For under that bow-tie is another bow-tie and
another bow-tie and another bow-tie and another
bow-tie. The clown pulls the bow-ties out faster and
faster from his shirt and when he has finished with
the bow-ties, he starts to take off jackets: striped

43

ones on top of checked ones on top of polka-dotted ones on top of patterned ones on top of flowered ones on top of plain ones on top of woven ones on top of knitted ones on top of wrinkled ones on top of smooth ones on top of . . . And after the jackets come the trousers and after the trousers come the shoes and after the shoes come the socks and after the socks . . .

Where has the Moon got to, where is the King?

'Help, help!' calls Annelie.

'Catch that ugly girl!' screeches a shrill voice and there is the Frock Woman on a snow-white horse. 'Catch that girl over there, she's stolen my shoes.'

All the trapezes together squeak the Swing's song. 'Yeeeow, yeeeow, wood and rope.'

Annelie stumbles out of the tent. She runs straight through the hedge and away, away, into the dark fields.

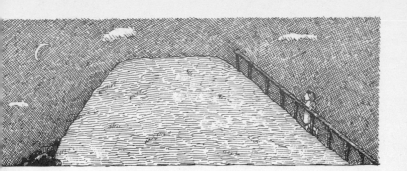

Chapter 9

At last the hubbub behind her dies down, but she doesn't stop running. The Moon and the King are nowhere to be seen. She climbs over fences and jumps across ditches, some of them so wide that it takes a count of three before she lands on the other side. In the distance she can see a dyke, just like the dyke where Grandma lives. Perhaps it is the very same dyke and she is going in the direction of Grandma's house.

Nine wooden steps with a handrail on the left-hand side lead upwards. On top of the dyke she finds herself standing between land and sea. She can see nobody on the land and no one out at sea. It is low tide and big stones are sticking out of the water.

Annelie starts to clamber down the dyke on the sea side, but the rocky slope is too slippery and she stays away from the edge. Down there, deep in the water, is Snatchweed Harry from Grandma's song.

45

If he can get hold of you he drags you down to the bottom by your legs. Annelie can hear the horrible song about the Tiger's Jaws inside her head.

'Quiet!' she says to her head, but the Head doesn't listen and just keeps on singing and humming:

> Annelie must go to sleep,
> Or else the plants upstairs will creep,
> Dragon Tree and Tiger's Jaws.
> In the water waits cold death,
> In the dark don't tarry,
> Twelve-teeth, Ten-toes there do lurk,
> They and Snatchweed Harry,
> Little horns and cloven feet,
> Black their tails and paws.
> Annelie must go to sleep,
> Or else the plants upstairs will creep,
> Dragon Tree and Tiger's Jaws.

Annelie gives her head a smack. 'That's enough! Be quiet!'

'I shall sing what I please,' says the Head. 'I shall sing and think whatever I please.'

'But you're mine,' says Annelie.

'Not at all, you are far more mine,' says the Head. 'You do what I think.' And the Head starts singing the song all over again.

Annelie smacks and smacks the Head and cries because it hurts.

Now the Head gets cross. 'No whining, please, it upsets me, no whining and no snivelling. I can do without swollen red eyes, a running nose and blotchy cheeks.'

'I'll stop if you stop singing,' says Annelie.

'Let's stop together, then,' says the Head.

And so they do.

Still no trace of the Moon.

Annelie sits down to wait at the top of the slope. She can't tell which side Grandma's village is.

The water laps gently against the big stones and pulls back between the narrow crevices with a sucking sound. There on the stones, under the slippery seaweed, live crabs and starfish. Annelie has often seen them dart away when she comes down with Grandma looking for winkles.

'Snatchweed Harry,' she calls, 'Snatchweed

Harry, let's have a look at you.' She's not frightened of him because she is sitting too high up for his clutching fingers. 'Snatchweed Harry, Snatchweed Harry, please come and see me. Snatchweed Harry, Snatchweed Harry, let's have a look.'

'Come closer, then, closer, closer, closer, then,' sounds a voice from out of the water.

'I'm not allowed to.'

'So many things are not allowed.'

'What else isn't allowed?'

'Telling lies is not allowed and singing nasty, lying songs is not allowed.'

'But who's been telling lies?'

'Anyone who sings songs about a Dragon Tree and a Tiger's Jaws. There isn't any such thing as a Dragon Tree or a Tiger's Jaws.'

'And what about Twelve-teeth and Ten-toes, then?'

'They exist all right, but they don't have any horns or tails and certainly no cloven feet. They are people. You are a ten-toe yourself, and a twelve-tooth.'

That makes Annelie sit up.

They are people and she's not afraid of people.

'And what about Snatchweed Harry, does he exist?'

'Oh, I do, I do,' says Snatchweed Harry and climbs out of the water and onto the stones. He is green and his arms and fingers are yards long. They nearly touch Annelie's feet. In a flash she pulls herself a little higher up the slope.

'And what do you think of me?' asks Snatchweed Harry.

'All right, not as bad as I thought.'

'And I can sing like a dream,' says Snatchweed Harry. 'That makes a lot of difference, at least most of the time it does.'

'Does what?'

'A good turn. Or as you would be done by. Listen.' He wraps his arms a few times around himself and sings to the beat of the waves:

> Lovey, lovey, lovey, love,
> Snatchweed Harry's little dove,
> Come down below, come down to me,
> Over my wave-steps into the sea,
> Down to my riddlemeree.

And Snatchweed Harry sings his song so sweetly

that without thinking Annelie starts sliding a little
lower down the slope.

> Lovey, Lovey, come with me,
> Come down to Snatchweed in the sea.

Lower, lower, lower.

And then! A hand grabs hold of her, but not by
her legs, no, by her hair and that hand pulls her up
the dyke. Suddenly there is a lot of light,
Snatchweed Harry slithers away from it, but Annelie
can still just see his slimy green body full of tendrils
and wattles and warts, with fishbones and birds'
legs and feathers sticking out of his crinkly hair.
From his mouth hangs a fish's tail. It is the Moon
who has come to her rescue. 'I can't leave you alone
for a single moment,' he says.

Snatchweed Harry ducks under the water.

'So lo-hong,' he calls from the deep, 'so-ho
lo-hong, we'll stay go-hood friends, fri-he-hends,
fri-he-hends . . .'

'You're talking through your green hat, you eerie
green weed!' says the Moon. 'So long as I'm around,
you'll never get Annelie, never, never, never!'

Chapter 10

They walk in a southerly direction and meet the Mouseking on the way.

'What kept you so long?' he asks. 'I've been there already.'

'Where have you been already?'

'Where we're going, of course.'

'And where are we going?'

'You know perfectly well,' says the Mouseking.

'But how do you know what no one knows except me?' persists the Moon.

Annelie stamps her feet.

'You're starting all over again. We're meant to be going to Grandma's house.'

'No, we're there already,' says the Moon.

To the right of them are the village houses.

Quickly the Moon peers through the windows.

'What can you see?' asks Annelie.

'When they have curtains I can't see anything,' says the Moon. 'But wait a minute.'

He climbs a bit higher into the sky so that all at
once a long glittering pathway of light falls across
the sea from the big stones to the horizon.

'What a lovely path!' cries Annelie. 'I'd love to
walk along it.'

'Yes, do-hooo!' says Snatchweed Harry's voice
from the sea.

'No, don't!' warns the Moon from the sky.

'She'd need her head examined if she did,' says
the Mouseking.

From far up in the sky the Moon sends down
long, thin rays of light, and with his threads of light
he lifts up the fronts of the houses.

Now Annelie can look inside at all the little rooms
and passages and stairs. All the houses are slightly
different, but all the people look the same, because
they are sleeping. In Grandma's house she can see
the bed with the little bars and under the eiderdown
she can see herself. She is fast asleep.

'How can that be? How can I be lying there when
I'm standing here?'

'That's easy,' says the Moon. He lets the
housefronts drop down again. They fall back neatly

52

into place with a soft thud. 'If you weren't lying asleep there, then you wouldn't be dreaming that you're standing here.'

'She could be lying asleep anywhere and be dreaming about standing here,' says the Mouseking. 'She could just as easily be lying asleep in her own bed back in the town and be dreaming about standing here.'

'Don't be tiresome,' says the Moon. 'Anyway, here I am back again. Did you see what I did? Houses are just like clothes. People put them on like coats. Sometimes a house fits nicely and sometimes it doesn't fit at all.'

'You're normally on your own inside your clothes when you've got them on,' says the Mouseking, 'but it's a bit lonely in a house when you're inside it all alone.'

'You're always thinking up things like that,' grumbles the Moon.

Annelie stops. 'I want to go home,' she whispers. 'Oh, I do so want to go home.'

'I'll take you there!' calls a voice from the sea and a green finger beckons.

The Moon rushes down the dyke and stamps on the finger. The finger disappears.

'We've just been to your home,' says the Moon.

'But I want to go home to my own home, I want to go home.'

'If that's what you want, then we'll go. Haven't I been asking you all along where you want to go?'

The Moon hoists the sail. Annelie and the Mouseking climb on board.

'Will it take long?' asks Annelie.

'No,' says the Moon. 'Look, can you see that black hole up there in the sky between the stars? That's where I really ought to be tonight.'

'Won't you get into trouble?' asked the Mouseking.

'Everyone is entitled to a holiday,' says the Moon.

The wind blows into the sail. Gone is the sea and gone the little houses by the dyke. The moonboat is already over a town.

Annelie hangs over the railing. 'I can see the school,' she calls out. 'I can see the recreation ground. I can see our house!'

And there it is, her very own home.

54

A light is on somewhere upstairs.

'Somebody's at home! Mummy's at home! Daddy's at home!'

'It's only the light in the bathroom,' says the Moon, 'and that's always on unless the bulb is broken.'

There are no flowers on the window-sills, no flowers in any of the rooms.

'Do you want to go in?' asks the Moon.

Annelie shakes her head. The darkness behind the flowerless windows frightens her. The house is her home and yet it isn't like her home. It is empty and when somewhere is empty, Swings and Frock Women take over. 'No,' she says.

'Then it's my turn to say where to go,' cries the King. 'I've actually been kept waiting for far too long already, since a King should always have precedence.'

'Where to, then?' asks the Moon.

'To the palace, of course,' says the Mouse with the Painted Moustache. 'I want to go to a proper palace, because I am the King.'

Chapter 11

Grandma is wearing a pink nightgown. Her grey
hair hangs down her back in a short plait.

'Is it daytime yet, Grandma?'

'No, not yet. But you've been coughing so, child.
What's the matter? I hope you're not sickening for
something.'

'Who's sickening for something?' says Annelie.
'The King? That's a shame, just as we're setting off
for the palace.'

'Goodness, how hot your hands are, child, and
you cheeks are burning, too.'

'I'm so thirsty, Grandma.'

'How could this have happened? Did you go out
without your coat?'

Annelie can't remember. She drinks some water
but her thirst won't go away.

'Does Snatchweed Harry live behind the dyke,
Grandma?'

'Oh, yes, wherever there's deep water.'

56

'Even in the ditch?'

'Even in the ditch. You're sick, child, I'll ring the doctor in the morning.'

'Come on now, stop being tiresome,' calls the Mouseking. 'I've been doing what you want long enough.'

Off they fly to a white town with turrets and domes.

'There's the palace,' says the Moon.

Annelie claps her hands. 'What a beautiful town!'

There is a broad river between overhanging trees and they land by a bridge that has statues on both of its parapets. They are statues of angels.

And the palace is round. Two sentries stand in the gateway.

'Make way for the King!' cries the King.

The sentries step aside and the gate swings open all by itself.

Inside the round wall lies a round courtyard with a smaller fortress right in the middle. There are more sentries and another gate and yet another courtyard with a fortress right in the middle.

They step through the third gate into a large hall.

Here, too, everything is round. People are walking
about in the hall as if there were no furniture in it.
They could be walking about outside, and the hall
could be a street or a square, because there are
brightly lit shop windows all around them. But the
floor is made of wood, not paving stones.

Behind a curtain to the left of the gate there is a
small door with a key in the lock. Annelie recognizes
the door and knows what's on the other side: the
long, narrow cupboard in which the apples are
stored for the winter. She can smell them through
the keyhole.

'That's the apple store,' she says to the Moon.

'This looks more like a town than like a palace,'
says the King. 'But then again, it looks more like
Annelie's house than like a town.'

'Hush,' whispers the Moon. He nods his head in
the direction of the shoppers. And there is the Frock
Woman going by carrying a dozen parcels.

'How can she be here now?' asks Annelie
anxiously. 'She was at the circus.'

'Let's get out of here before she spots us,' says the
King. 'I don't much like this palace anyway.'

58

They disappear into the apple store as quietly as possible and lock the door behind them. The apples have dark spots on them that are quickly growing bigger. It's hard not to step on the rotting apples.

'This isn't a storeroom, it's a secret exit,' says the Moon. He lights the way for Annelie and the King.

The wooden floor makes way for grey stones, and the walls are stone as well. It is cold and damp and dark in the storeroom.

Annelie is growing more and more nervous. She knows that the Frock Woman has found out where she is and will be coming after her. She runs ahead of the Moon across the slippery cobblestones, her outstretched hands touching the damp walls on either side. Is that the Frock Woman she can hear behind her? She can see small openings high up on the walls and now and then there is a niche with something moving inside. An animal? A person?

'Not so fast,' calls the King. 'My paws are only little, even if there *are* four of them.'

The Moon lifts him up, then picks Annelie up as well.

'There's the end of the passage,' he says.

And it's true. There they are, standing in bright sunlight at the top of a wide, white staircase. And there are flowers. In Grandma's blue vase.

'Where am I?' asks Annelie.

'You are in the living room, child,' says Grandma. 'I've put you down on the settee.'

Annelie looks round. She is lying on Grandma's settee with her own pillows and eiderdown. There are flowers in the blue vase on the table, and the sun in shining brightly in the glass panes in the corner cupboard.

Chapter 12

The doctor comes. She is a lady, and has little grey curls. She carries a bag with cough sweets inside.

'Take a deep breath,' says the doctor as she listens to Annelie's back and Annelie's chest with something cold.

'Stay under the blankets and on no account get out of bed. I'm going to give you a nice mixture to drink, all right?'

The doctor's face is round and friendly and a bit shiny.

'Do you know the Moon?' asks Annelie.

'Yes, I know the moon, of course I know the moon,' says the doctor.

Perhaps she is related to the Moon, a niece or an aunt.

The doctor and Grandma are having a talk in the kitchen. It is taking a long time.

'I say, my moustache could do with a lick of paint,' says the Mouseking.

'What are you doing here?' cries Annelie. 'Grandma will be back any minute and then she'll catch you.'

'Oh, no, she won't,' says the Mouseking cockily. 'No one can catch me, I'm far too quick. And anyway I know how to sit completely still, as still as a . . . well, absolutely still, and then you could easily take me for an ink-well or a piece of cake.'

'Oh, no,' says Annelie. 'Not with a green moustache, you couldn't. Come on, hurry up!'

But the mouse goes straight on sitting there.

And here comes Grandma now. She tucks Annelie's blankets in more tightly.

'I'm going to give your Daddy a ring and ask him to come and see you,' she says.

'And Mummy, too,' says Annelie with a contented sigh.

'If you ask me, this can't be the depths of the night,' says the Mouseking conversationally. He is running across the flowered bedspread in full view of Grandma, who is sitting in her armchair. But how peculiar! Clouds are starting to rise up from out of the eiderdown and Grandma's face can only just be

made out above them. The Mouseking dances to and fro in front of the depths of the night.

'No, this can't possibly be the depths of the night. Out of the question!'

'Why do you say that?' asks Annelie. Grandma's face has now disappeared behind the clouds.

'It's broad daylight, so there's no way this can be the depths of the night.'

'That's true. But what else can it be? You're still the same old Mouse with the Painted Moustache that you were last night and I'm still the same old Annelie.'

'Aha, but is your second name "Of the Night", or let us say "O'Knight"? Is my second name "O'Knight"?'

'No, but . . .'

'I've got you there, haven't I?'

'Tell me, Mouse, what *is* your second name?'

'Well, that goes without saying. It's Mouseking.'

'And your first name?'

'Mouseking, of course.'

'So you're called Mouseking Mouseking?'

'Well, if you must know, my full name is Mouseking M. G. Mouseking.'

'What does the M. G. stand for?'

'It stands for Mouseking as well, naturally. It's the first and last letters with full stops after them. That's all.'

'And my name is Hank B. Hedgehog,' observes the Hedgehog, who is busy with a sledge. 'But my mother was called something quite different.'

'I shouldn't worry about that if I were you,' says the Mouseking, 'seeing that you stink and you can't even dance.'

'Oh, no? I'm as good a dancer as any hedgehog, and-a-one, and-a-two, and-a-one, two, three.' And Hank B., the hedgehog, puts down his sledge and twirls gracefully around.

'Oh, do sit down,' says the Mouseking. 'We've seen it all before.'

'You aren't being very nice to the Hedgehog,' hisses Annelie, 'you've hurt his feelings.'

'I'm never nice to hedgehogs,' says the Mouseking in a loud voice. 'Fancy that! Being nice to hedgehogs, whatever next?' He pulls her past the Hedgehog, who is still dancing about. 'My moustache needs doing in a hurry, it can't wait, you

can see the red through the green.'

In the Mouseking's little room Annelie paints the moustache a handsome green again.

Mouseking M. G. Mouseking looks at himself in the mirror. 'Now I am even Kingier,' he says.

They drink squash from the cupboard and eat cheese-rind from a tin. Annelie can see that the wedding shoes have been put under the mousebed.

'They're safer under a bed,' says the Mouseking. 'People only look for slippers under a bed. And now, Annelie, I have a surprise for you. Something just for you, just from me, something for an ordinary little girl from a Mouseking. Home-made and home-sung.'

The Mouseking stands up, wipes the crumbs of cheese from his chest and starts to sing in warm, heartfelt tones:

> Who sings the song, and-a-one, and-a-two,
> Of the little girl, and-a-one, two, three,
> She lives in a kingdom by the sea so blue . . .

Here the Mouseking interrupts himself: 'That's my kingdom, of course, you understand that, don't

you? I'll just start again.' He rearranges his tail
neatly by his side, coughs and sings:

Who sings the song, and-a-one, and-a-two,
Of the little girl, and-a-one, two, three,
She lives in a kingdom by the sea so blue,
And her name is Annelie.

Who sings the song so loud and bright,
Of that little girl, and-a-one, two, three,
She knows the Moon and the depths of the night,
And her name is Annelie.

Who sings the song both high and low,
Of that little girl, and-a-one, two, three,
Who asks for answers that only I know,
And her name is Annelie . . .

The mouse bows to the left and to the right and
then looks at Annelie, not best pleased. 'You might
have clapped at such a magnificent song.'

'Oh, I think it's lovely,' says Annelie, 'but it made
me cry, and I much prefer songs that make me
laugh.'

66

'You're a fine one,' grumbles the Mouseking. 'I suppose what you'd really like is something with a whole lot of hey-nonny-noes and tra-la-las. Well, you've come to the wrong place. A King doesn't sing rubbish, a King sings the better class of song, and that's always going to make you have a little weep, or better yet, sob your heart out. Just imagine if I stood about here hey-nonny-noing: my subjects would get the idea that everything was so hunkydory they could just sit around twiddling their thumbs all day. No, no, out of the question!'

'But I can't see any subjects. And this is a common-or-garden mousehole, not a palace. And you haven't got a crown or a lackey or a throne.'

The Mouseking flies into a rage. 'So that's all the thanks I get for treating someone to a home-made song! You have hurt my feelings, and since I am a reigning monarch, that is nothing short of treason.' He thumps the ground hard three times with his tail.

'Come on, Mouseking, don't upset yourself over nothing.'

'Over nothing! That takes the biscuit! And as for

saying I have no subjects, well, I've got plenty of
subjects! What's more, I've got an army! I'll teach
you to hurt my feelings.'

'Forward, march!' is heard in the distance.

Annelie leans out of the mousewindow and sees
Hank B. Hedgehog wearing an army cap on his
head. He is marching at the head of the troops.

'But those are the tea soldiers!' cries Annelie.

Chapter 13

'Those aren't your soldiers, they're my soldiers.
Grandma gave them to me!'

'They are marching for me because I am the King,
so there.'

'And who made you king? I did! You are nothing
but a mouse with a red moustache and I'll tell the
whole world about it if you don't stop that stupid
army.'

The King coughs and snorts and thumps his tail
on the floor. 'Let's negotiate,' he suggests. 'You
don't say anything and I'll keep the soldiers.'

'And what do I get out of that?'

'You won't have to go to prison.'

'No. Those are my tea soldiers and my tea soldiers
they remain.'

The King rushes over to the window. 'Who do
you belong to?' he bawls at the tea soldiers. 'To me,
your King, or to that girl over there? Who do you
belong to?'

'To the tea, to the tea, to the tea,' comes the answer.

Annelie and the Mouseking look at each other.

'Shall we be friends again?' asks the King. 'If I take really good care of your shoes, will you let the soldiers march for me?'

'All right,' says Annelie.

'Good! That's settled, then. Let's go and watch the parade,' cries the Mouseking.

They go outside and stand on a little platform under the window and take the salute. The tea soldiers march past in orderly ranks.

The Mouseking shakes his head. 'Something's gone wrong in the middle.'

Annelie can see it as well. 'One row's a bit wonky.'

'Mark time!' commands the Mouseking.

'Time!' bawls the Hedgehog, and all the tea soldiers shout out in unison: 'One! Two! One! Two!'

But somewhere in the middle of the rank and file is one soldier who is shouting: 'One, two, three! One, two, three!'

'Halt!' orders the King. 'Over here, soldier. You there.'

70

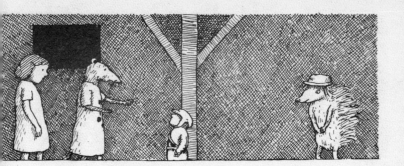

The soldier steps forward and salutes.

'Why are you shouting "one, two, three"?'

'Isn't that right, King?'

'Of course it isn't, you idiot. You are out of step.'

'I shouldn't have thought so, King. I have a very good sense of rhythm, my father was dancing master at court.'

The Mouseking is beginning to get hot under the collar. 'What sort of soldier are you? Just tell me this: if all the soldiers go "up arms!" or "at them!", what will you do?'

The soldier doesn't have to think long. 'I'll go "help , first aid, help, first aid"! Or at worst "strike me down", but you can only do that once.'

'This soldier is absolutely useless,' says the Mouseking to the Hedgehog. 'He's upsetting the rest. Get him an office job.'

The tea soldiers march off without the useless soldier, the rank and file as straight as a die.

The useless soldier follows the army with his eyes. 'I'm not made of tin, that's what it is,' he says. 'I'm a clay soldier, handpainted. I'm one of the old guard, I used to be one of this little girl's grandpa's toys. He

must have had a good hundred of us clay soldiers. One hundred strong, we were.'

'So where have the other ninety-nine got to?' asks the Mouseking, suddenly all ears. 'Stuck away in an old box, perhaps, or fallen in the heat of battle?'

'Drowned, every man jack of them,' says the useless soldier. 'This little girl's grandpa took my pals into the bath with him and that's where they perished.'

'Why was that?'

'It was the water, you see. They melted away. Mud, the whole lot mud at one fell swoop. I wasn't with them. To tell you the truth I'd gone missing a long time before. Under a stove.'

'A blessing in disguise,' says the Mouseking.

'A blessing!' shouts the useless soldier. 'You call that a blessing? Being the last of one hundred strong? Some blessing, that, ha, ha!' He walks off with his head held high.

Annelie watches him go. The clay soldier looks terribly lonely, quite lost without his ninety-nine brothers-in-arms.

The Mouseking bursts into song:

> Oh, what ails you, man of clay,
> You can't keep step or find the way,
> You march alone where no one may,
> Alone today.
>
> We were a hundred men all told,
> Now I am left out in the cold,
> Last of that hundred brave and bold,
> These men of old.

The song makes Annelie feel sad again, but the King says: 'Now we'll go and eat. We've got bullybeef and hardtack, and you can have as many mouthfuls as there are tea soldiers, or no, that's too simple, you can have as many mouthfuls as there are arms and legs and fingers and toes and nails and teeth in my whole army. Not forgetting the buttons on the coats of the drowned clay soldiers. Start counting, one, two, three . . .'

'I can't,' says Annelie, 'and I don't want to eat, I want a drink.'

Someone hands her a drink. Is it the Mouseking?

Or the clay soldiers? Can she really hear a car hooting nearby, just like Daddy's car? No, it can't be, she must be dreaming . . .

Chapter 14

'Where has the Moon got to? I can't see the Moon anywhere,' Annelie complains.

'You can't see the moon tonight. It's a moonless night,' explains Daddy, but it can't be Daddy, perhaps it's the clay soldier.

A moonless night and no light anywhere. Annelie has lost her way in the depths of the night. There are so many passages and each passage branches out into side-passages. She is getting frightened. The Frock Woman is sure to be prowling around in one of those passages or side-passages waiting to snatch the satin shoes. Annelie gropes her way forward. Her hand touches something warm and hairy. She screams with fright.

'Easy now, easy does it,' says Daddy, but it isn't Daddy, it's the Fox. He is holding a lantern up and the light shines on his red coat.

'Are you – are you the Fox from the depths of the night?'

The Fox nods and grins from pointed ear to
pointed ear.

'Little girl, would you care to visit my humble
abode? My humble home not far from here?'

Annelie doesn't know if she can trust the Fox. His
voice sounds like Daddy's voice, but he has rather
slanting eyes.

'I've got a beautiful home, it's the pride of the
neighbourhood,' says the Fox in a wheedling voice.

'All right, then,' says Annelie.

'You'll have to join the guided tour, of course, that
can't be helped, because rules are rules, aren't they?
But this is your lucky day! There's a special price
today for one day only. A mere one hundred hairs
for the whole guided tour, but mind you, absolutely
no tricks.'

'One hundred hairs, isn't that rather a lot?'

'A lot? For a guided tour? A mere trifle! Keep still,
I'll pluck them myself.'

Annelie lets the Fox have his way. 'Ouch!' she
says one hundred times.

'What's the matter, are you in pain?' asks the Fox,
speaking with Daddy's voice.

76

'Yes, I am, ouch, it hurts!'

The Fox bends closely over her, his flashing claws pull and pull, his tail is as hot as Grandma's electric fire.

'I'm so hot.'

Sometimes the clouds behind the Fox's lantern shift to one side and you can catch a sudden glimpse of Grandma's corner cupboard and of the flower-patterned knitting chair and of somebody who looks like Daddy and who strokes her forehead with something cool every so often.

'Ninety-nine, one hundred,' counts the Fox. 'That's that, the guided tour can begin.'

He takes his lantern and goes on ahead, all the while reeling off a long rigmarole in a proper guide's voice: 'Ladies and gentlemen, you will be aware that a foxhole can be very old indeed, sometimes as much as one hundred years old. Foxholes such as these were frequently dug out in the first instance by other animals, for example Badgers, who are exceptionally good at excavating holes. Nevertheless Badgers do not like to live by themselves and are only too happy to share their quarters, preferably

with a fox . . .' Suddenly the Fox stands still and
says in his normal voice: 'Incidentally, did you
notice the special way in which I was speaking?'

'Yes, I hardly recognized your voice.'

'I didn't mean that,' says the Fox impatiently.
'Didn't you notice all those words that people don't
manage to get their tongues around any more, such
as Exceptionally and Frequently and Nevertheless
and Preferably, you don't hear those words
nowadays, at most you might see them in books. I
know quite a lot of words like that, although I say so
myself. I know Likewise and Heretofore and
Notwithstanding. Be honest, you didn't know those,
did you?'

'I must have known them,' says Annelie, 'or else I
couldn't have dreamt them.'

'But do you ever use them?'

'No, of course I don't. People would laugh at me.'

'Exactly. I'll carry on with the guided tour, then.
This particular hole is the home of a Badger and a
Fox, that's myself of course, a Polecat and a Wild
Cat. We four are the main tenants, but you'll find
the odd sub-tenant here and there as well. People of

no importance. If they don't behave, the Badger and I kick them out.'

'Who are they, these animals, er, people, of no importance?'

'Rabbits, Little Owls, an Otter, I believe, and a Mallard.'

'No, er, Frock Woman?'

'Most certainly not,' says the Fox. 'The very idea! There's no place here for Frock Women, that's all we're short of. Well, here we are then, please step inside my humble abode.'

Annelie would rather not have to step inside the humble abode, it's stuffy and cramped inside, there are long rows of mouse tails strung along the walls, the floor is paved with claws and beaks, and the remains of hideous meals are lying about all over the place.

'Nice, isn't it? And elegant, don't you think?' asks the Fox. 'That lot cost me a pretty penny, believe me. You can certainly see that we're not riffraff down here and that we're comfortably off. But then this hole has been in our family since 1880. Do sit down, please.'

79

Chapter 15

The foxhole must be situated right in the middle of the depths of the night. Not a breath of air has been able to find its way into the humble abode. Annelie can feel her sleeves sticking to her arms. She has been sitting waiting on a stool for several minutes. The Fox has sat down on his tail and is busy with the hundred hairs. His claws are clicking softly. He is plaiting the hairs into a rope.

'Fox, why are you plaiting my hair?'

'To make a strong cord.'

'Fox, why are you making a strong cord?'

'To tie somebody up.'

'Fox, who do you want to tie up?' shrieks Annelie.

'There was a little girl and she had a little curl . . . And she had a nice name, a lovely name, and that name is . . .'

'No! No! No!'

The clouds move away. There is Daddy with his arms stretched out towards her.

'Come, child, come, my darling.'

'Come, child, let me tie you up,' says the Fox, interrupting.

'No! No! No!'

'Don't you want me to tie you up with this beautiful rope? No? Well, all right then, we'll have a chat about it later. Meanwhile I'll let you go, but you must do something in return. You must hand Mouseking M. G. Mouseking over to me, that old rascal.'

'The Mouseking is my friend!'

'Don't be tiresome. Mice are there to be eaten.'

'Not the Mouseking, not a mouse who, who . . . who sings songs.'

The Fox looks up in surprise. 'Sings songs? Does he do that, the old scallywag? Hm, well, that rather changes things. I am a patron of the Arts and as such am exceedingly loath to lay so much as a finger on a musical mouse. Pity. But there it is. He is a colleague. I belong to a group of singers myself. We perform the better class of song.'

'That's what the Mouseking does, too,' says Annelie.

'Oh, does he? Well, one better class of song is quite different from the next. I'm sure you'll agree once you've heard us. And hear us you shall. Then you'll appreciate that the Mouseking is nothing but a caterwauler. It so happens that our group is about to give a concert under my inspired leadership. It's all part, so to speak, of the guided tour that you've already paid for. That means you have a more or less perfect right to come to the concert. But for the refreshments during the interval I must ask for a further fifteen hairs. Just keep your head still.'

'Ouch! Ouch! Ouch!'

The Polecat, the Badger and the Wild Cat come to find out what all the noise is about.

'Who's squealing like that? Have you caught a sucking-pig, yum-yum?'

'No, an audience for our concert.'

'Are we going to eat her up after the finale, then, is she for our supper?'

'Wait a minute, I know her,' says the Wild Cat. 'Her name is Annelie.'

The Wild Cat is Glum, her own cat that ran away.

'Oh, Glum, dear Glum, where have you been?'

'Seeing the big wide world, I was fed up with
things.'

'We looked for you everywhere, we thought you
were dead, oh, we cried so much when you didn't
come back.'

'Don't exaggerate,' says Glum. 'Have you brought
me anything? Liver? Heart?'

'I didn't know you were here.'

'A fine excuse,' snaps Glum. He is no longer
friendly, there is a shifty look in his eyes.

'The concert's about to begin, the gong has gone,'
calls the Fox.

'What gong?' asks the Badger. 'I didn't hear a
gong.'

'Nor did I,' says the Polecat. He stinks.

'If I say the gong has gone, then the gong has
gone,' says the Fox. 'The concert is beginning.'

'Wait a minute, wait a minute,' calls the Badger.
He runs down the passage and comes back a
moment later. 'I had quite forgotten to spray on my
scent. How do I smell now?'

'Like a badger who has sprayed himself with
scent,' says the Fox.

The four animals climb onto a small platform, pick some hats and short walking sticks out of a box and bow to Annelie. Annelie claps.

The Badger takes a small step forward. 'The programme is as follows: first we shall perform "The Song of the Great Master of the Hounds", next we shall sing "Tiger's Jaws", and in conclusion, by popular request, we shall give a rendering of "Round My Humble Home the Poplars Grow".'

The Polecat begs to differ. 'Let's sing "Rose, Fragrant Rose".'

'No,' say the Fox, the Wild Cat and the Badger.

The four singers line up next to each other, one shoulder turned towards the audience, holding their hats in one hand and their walking sticks in the other, and sing:

> Is there a bridge,
> From here to there?
> A bridge of stone,
> A bridge of wood?
> Tiddleypom?
> Tiddleypom, the wind doth blow,

And a sparrow is no swan,
If ever the ice in the sea dries up,
Where shall we go to drown?
Tiddleypom?
Tiddleypom, I'm warning you,
The piper you must pay,
The child is sick, the child is dead,
The wagon has come to take her away.
Tiddleypom!
Were there a bridge from there to here,
A bridge of rope or perhaps of lead,
That old black wagon would not have come,
And the youngest child would not be dead.
Tiddleypom?
Tiddleypom!

'I still think that "Rose, Fragrant Rose" would have been better,' whines the Polecat.

'You'd be better off keeping your trap shut about being fragrant,' says the Fox. 'You're the last person to let the word fragrant pass your lips.'

'While we are on the subject of things passing our lips,' begins the Wild Cat, 'is it true that she knows

the Mouseking?'

All four of them look at Annelie.

'Yes, she knows him, the old villain, and it appears that he's taken to singing songs.'

'So what? It'll only take a moment for me to make sure he never sings again,' grins the Wild Cat. 'Or sings out of tune, anyway.'

He steps down from the platform and comes up to Annelie, his tail swishing to and fro over his back. 'Let you and me go and pay a call on good old Mouseking,' he purrs, 'and then you can introduce him to me properly. I'm sure you won't mind doing that for me, for your old Glum.'

'But you'll eat him up,' stammers Annelie.

'Not straight away, I won't,' says the Wild Cat, looking sly. 'Oh, no, not straight away.'

'No, indeed, that would not be a sensible move,' the Fox agrees. 'First we must see to it that he calls all his subjects together for an interesting guided tour followed by a lovely concert. What a splendid time those little creatures will have, there is so little fun otherwise in their drab, grey little lives.'

The Badger and the Polecat nod vigorously.

'I shan't do it,' says Annelie.

'That's most unwise.' The Fox toys with the cord of hair. 'Because if you won't play the game with us then we'll just have to summon the Frock Woman, won't we?'

The plait swings slowly to and fro. 'Well? Have you thought it over?'

'I shan't do it, I shan't do it!'

Step by step, the four singers advance on Annelie, one shoulder turned towards her, as they sing softly and in unison about the bridge and the old black wagon.

Chapter 16

Sometimes it is day and sometimes it is night. The clouds in the foxhole dissolve and there is Daddy or Grandma and now and then the doctor with her round face.

'Go and talk to the Moon,' pleads Annelie.

She is at the mercy of the four singers, their prisoner, and if she doesn't betray the Mouseking then they'll set the Frock Woman on her.

'Please go and talk to the Moon.'

The Fox is being very friendly to her, speaking in a soothing, kindly voice, but all the while he is tying her up with the cord and knotting the hairs on her head one by one to the mousetails above her so that whenever she moves she has to cry out with the pain.

'Are you going to take us to the Mouseking, that old swindler?'

'No, no no!'

'Then we'll fetch you-know-who.'

And so it continues, all day and all night.

'Will you do as we say?'

'I cannot betray a friend.'

'Be quiet, I can hear something. Shut up a moment,' hisses the Wild Cat. 'Someone is coming.'

'The Frock Woman? Already?' asks the Badger, sounding slightly annoyed. 'She's too early.'

'Has the Frock Woman ever had eighty little feet?'

'Not that I know of.'

The four singers go into conference. Annelie can hear it herself now, the brisk tapping of little feet in the foxhole courtyard with its paving of claws and beaks.

'Attention!' shouts a familiar voice. It is Mouseking M. G. Mouseking himself at the head of his army.

'That's unfair, that's cheating, forty against four!' screams the Fox. 'Just what you'd expect of that old crook.'

'Untie her, then at least we'll be five,' says the Polecat craftily.

As fast as they can, they untie Annelie. It's quite a hard job.

'Remember, you're one of us now!' warns the Fox.

But Annelie makes a run for it, straight to the Mouseking's army.

'Bah, she's nothing but a turncoat,' says the Badger.

And the four of them burst into song, so badly out of tune that the Mouseking stuffs his paws into his ears and sounds the retreat.

'What a dirty trick,' he sighs when they are back safe and well in the mousehole drinking squash and eating cheese-rind. The satin wedding shoes are now standing among the glasses in the cupboard.

'A place of honour,' the Mouseking explains. 'Those shoes belong to a Loyal Friend. You refused to betray us.'

'How did you get hold of that picture of Cinderella?' asks Annelie in surprise. She can see the brown fox-marks clearly, the doves and the peas, and suddenly she is no longer in the King's hole, but in Grandma's kitchen. Daddy is carrying

her in his arms, the eiderdown wrapped tightly
around her.

'Where are we going?'

'I'm taking you to the car,' says Daddy.

'Are we going home? Back to Mummy?' She can
feel the car droning and humming and whirring
along. 'Where are we going?'

Why is everything so white? This isn't the depths
of the night, nor is it the place where the Moon
always waits for her. Are they at the North Pole? Or
in a desert? Is everything made of sand? 'But we
were going home,' she thinks, 'we were in the car.'

She can see the Mouseking's head. His mouth
says: 'No, no, no, no, that's out of the question, you
know that. There's no one at home and you're sick.
If they had to call in the doctor then you must be
sick.'

Annelie is lying in a white bed in a white room.
She has a white blanket with a white counterpane.
A white lady and two white gentlemen are standing
beside her. Daddy has gone and Grandma has gone.
The Mouseking has gone. The eiderdown has gone.

'My eiderdown . . .' Annelie can't speak. 'Now I won't be able to get back to the depths of the night any more,' she thinks, 'not without the eiderdown.'

The white gentleman does something to her arm. She sinks right through the bottom of the white bed, deep, deep, deep.

'Ssssh,' whispers the Mouseking, 'it's me. I would never leave a Loyal Friend in the lurch.'

'Where am I?'

'Where I am, of course,' says the Mouseking testily. 'That's plain enough, isn't it?'

'But where are you?'

'With me,' says the Moon.

'Moon, I can't see you, Moon!'

'Take a good look.'

And there right in the middle of all the whiteness she can see the Moon like an inkblot on a sheet of paper. He puts Annelie in his boat and they sail away out of the white room and into a black tunnel.

'It's getting dark!'

'What do you expect? The dark side of the Moon means what it says.'

'I can't see anything any more.'
'Can you see the stars?'
'No, everything is so black.'
'The stars are extinct, that's why. Can you see the holes?'
'No.'
'That's because they're black holes.'
'Oh, Moon, I'm scared of the dark, let's go back.'
'Back to that white place?'
'Yes, back there.'
The Dark Moon puts the boat about and they sail out of the tunnel.
'Can you see anything yet?'
'No, no, everything is so white.'
'Can you see the sand of the dunes?'
'Sand? I can't see any sand.'
'That's because it's white sand. Can you see the doves?'
'What doves? I can't see any doves.'
'That's because they are white doves.'
'Cinderella's doves?'
She can't see any doves, but whose is that nice

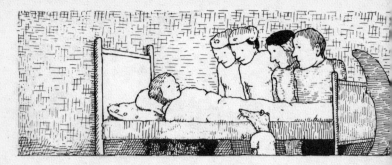

face among the white walls and beds? 'Are you Cinderella?'

'No, I am the Sister.'

'Oh. And where is the other sister? There were two, weren't there?'

'She'll be back very soon,' says the one Sister.

'And the stepmother? Am I in Cinderella's house?'

'Yes, this is the hospital,' say the Sisters. They nod and smile.

'You're in hospital,' say Daddy and Grandma.

'This is the hospital,' say the Moon and the Mouseking.

'I'll get you even in hospital,' says the Frock Woman from under the bed.

'People only look for slippers under a bed.'

'Hospital, hospital, white wagons, black wagons,' sing the four singers.

Everyone says she's in hospital, so it must be true.

Chapter 17

Every time something annoying happens, Grandma
says: 'There now, hospital is worse.'

Hospital is worse! Worse than broken vases,
worse than boiled-over milk. And now Annelie is in
hospital herself.

She doesn't know what to make of it, everything
is strange, though the depths of the night is lying
there as usual under the thin hospital blankets. She
noticed that immediately, on the very first day,
though it hasn't done her much good. She is too
scared to go in without the Moon. The four singers
are in there somewhere lying in wait for her, and the
Frock Woman is in there somewhere, too.

Annelie doesn't know how long she has been
lying in the white bed, all she knows is that Mummy
hasn't been to visit her in all that time. What does
that mean? That Mummy is sick herself? That
Mummy is a long way away? That Mummy is –
dead? No! Not dead. Not that. She needs to know,

but no one will tell her when she asks. 'I'll have to go and look for her,' thinks Annelie. 'I'll have to go and look for her myself.'

One night when the Sister has left, she gets out of bed. She peeps round the door to the left and to the right. There is a long corridor with doors everywhere and strange sounds are coming from behind the doors. Might there be a Fox behind one of the closed doors? Or a Frock Woman? She starts down the corridor as fast as she can and then, all of a sudden, she notices that she can take off from the floor. With every step she floats a bit further through the air. 'This is really very easy,' thinks Annelie. 'I'll have to tell Grandma about it one day.'

The floating gets better and better. Taking a big jump she flies down the stairs without more ado, through the ground-floor corridors, round corners, over the head of the night porter and into the open air outside. She makes swimming movements with her arms, gathering quite a bit of speed. Below her lies the town with all its little lights. If she wanted to, she could fly home, but she knows that Mummy isn't there and she'd rather the Moon came along

with her to the empty house. Before she knows
what is happening, she finds herself flying in the
direction of Grandma's village. She has to cross the
sea, the dunes, the woods, and the circus meadow.

The tent is still up. She can see the animals in
their cages through a hole in the roof. There are no
people about. Everyone is asleep, except for the
clown, who is doing something beside the tent all on
his own. He is piling boxes up on top of each other,
big boxes and small boxes, in all shapes and colours.

'What are you doing, clown?' Annelie calls.

'You can see for yourself. I am filling space up
with boxes,' says the clown. 'I've still got the rest of
space to fill tonight, the rest of the universe, the
cosmos, you might say. And not just a little bit full,
oh, no, it's going to have to be absolutely chock-a-
block full.'

'But you can't do that with boxes,' says Annelie.
'There aren't enough of them to do it. And the
universe isn't square, is it?'

The clown starts walking round the boxes, kicking
them. 'That's no good then. I'll have to fill the
universe up with balls instead. Footballs, tennis

balls, beach balls, all the kind of balls there are.'

'But, clown, there aren't enough balls either. And the universe isn't round. Or is it?'

'What a fusspot you are,' scolds the clown. 'All right, I won't use balls, I've thought of something better. I'll fill the universe up with apples. Apples, apples, apples! Since the universe is nothing but a great big apple core, anyway, nothing else will do.'

And he starts to pile up apples at tremendous speed. It's a mystery where they come from, but there they are, and in double-quick time the apple mountain has grown higher than the circus tent. And it is growing not only higher and higher, but broader and broader too.

Annelie swims furiously with her arms, trying to keep ahead of the apples which are following close on her heels. Luckily, the dyke isn't far away now, there is Grandma's little house, there is the green car. But the apples are catching up with her. She jumps over the gable roof down into the street and creeps inside the car. She didn't know she could drive, but the car starts with a growl and she steers it with great ease past the familiar houses and

shops. Immediately behind her the village disappears under an avalanche of apples.

Somewhere behind the mountain the clown is shouting:

Apple, sweet apple, with cheek round and red,
I'll honour and keep you,
If you will me wed.
Be true to me and I'll give you a treat,
But if you betray me, oh, apple so sweet,
You'll end up in the pan
As a pancake or flan.

The stars are disappearing behind the apple mountain. If things go on like this, the Moon will never be able to come down again.

Annelie stops the car and looks around. Apples. Are Grandma and Daddy buried inside under a pile of apples? Then they'll suffocate, no one can breathe under so many apples.

Annelie turns the green car round and drives straight for the apple mountain. The bottom layer is soft and mushy and the car easily tunnels a way through the wet mass. She drives past house after

house, but which is Grandma's door? Then the car
stalls and will move neither forwards nor backwards
any more. The brownish apple pulp is pressing
against the windows.

'Help!' screams Annelie.

The roof and the sides of the car start to close in,
and the space inside is becoming smaller and
smaller. The apples are squashing the car.

'Help! Help!'

'Come on, now, just a bite or two,' says the Sister.
She is sitting in the middle of all the apples.

'Open your mouth. You really must have a little
something to eat. Lovely apple sauce.'

'No apple sauce!' Annelie tries to say, but her
mouth is already full.

'And another bite,' says the Sister.

> One, I stood on a stone. And another bite!
> Two, I broke my bone. And another bite!
> Three, it made me sore. And another bite!
> Four, I'll do it no more. And another bite!

'What won't I do any more?' asks Annelie.

'Bite,' says the Sister.

Chapter 18

At long last the Moon has appeared, dark but well.
The hospital is quiet, though people snuffle and sigh
and groan behind every door. The Night Sister is
sitting by her small light. She cannot see the Moon
because he is too dark.

'Are you coming?'

The satin shoes are lying in the boat.

'How did those get there?' asks Annelie.

'The Mouseking sent them with his best regards.
He couldn't come tonight, his army has revolted.
They want more bullybeef and less hardtack. And
on top of that they want tea three times a day.'

'Where shall we go, Moon?'

'Wherever you like.'

'I'd like to go home.'

'There's no one at home.'

'Even so, I'd like to go home.'

'Third time lucky,' says the Dark Moon. 'But
remember: three, it made me sore, four, I'll do it no

more. This is the last time.'

The light in the bathroom is still on.

'I want to know where Mummy is,' says Annelie. 'She has to be somewhere! Daddy is at Grandma's, but where is Mummy, where has Mummy gone?'

Annelie walks around the house and then she puts on the satin shoes and starts ringing the neighbours' door-bells. 'Where is my Mummy?' she asks.

'Not at home,' reply the neighbours on the left side, and the neighbours on the right side, and Tanya's aunt, and Fred's father, and the doctor's wife, and the schoolmistress.

'Gone,' they say in the shops, in the streets, in the parks.

'But she has to be somewhere,' groans Annelie. She is wobbling on her high heels, she can't go any further.

The Moon pulls her on board his boat. 'We're not likely to find out anything here.'

'Please look for her then, Moon! You can shine in everywhere.'

'I can't do any shining right now,' says the Moon,

'you can see that, I'm the Dark Moon right now and that's the wrong phase altogether.'

'Then I want to go to the dyke. To Snatchweed Harry.'

'What do you want with that eerie green weed?'

'I just want to ask him a question.'

They sail before the wind, west-south-west. The sky is full of stars, but stars give hardly any light.

'We're there,' says the Moon. He can tell where he is even in the dark.

Annelie steps out on to the top of the dyke. The Moon clutches hold of her and digs a sharp nail into her arm. 'Mind you don't do anything silly now!'

'Snatchweed Harry! Snatchweed Harry!' calls Annelie. She kicks the shoes off and lowers herself down the dyke, careful not to slip on the wet grass.

'Not all the way down!' warns the Moon anxiously.

'Snatchweed Harry?'

'Here I am, he-here.' Lapping sounds come from beneath the stones. 'Is that my dear, my very dearest Annelie?'

'Snatchweed Harry, if I come any closer, you

won't grab hold of me, will you?'

'You know very well that I shall!'

'But will you tell me the truth?'

'You know very well that I never tell lies.'

'Have you got my Mummy?'

'No, I haven't, more's the pity,' says Snatchweed Harry.

'Have you got my Grandpa?'

'That one I've got, ha, ha, ha, that one I've got.'

'Have you got Aunt Lydia?'

'Her too, her too. Aren't I the clever one? No one could ever have expected it, but I got her and now I have her and I mean to keep her.'

'Have you got our old teacher?'

'Oh, yes.'

'Have you got Mummy?'

'Not that one, no, no, not that one.'

'Thank you very much,' says Annelie, and climbs back up the dyke.

'Here, I say, are you leaving already? Aren't you going to play with me?'

Annelie shakes her head. 'You know very well that I'm not.'

'That's true, but we can always live in hope. So long then, dear Annelie.'

'Goodbye, Snatchweed Harry.' She steps into the boat and waves in the dark.

As they sail away she can hear Snatchweed Harry's wistful voice getting fainter and fainter.

'So long, so-ho lo-hong, so-ho lo-ho-hong . . .'

Chapter 19

'Are you satisfied now?' asks the Moon. 'Is that what you wanted to know?'

'Yes,' says Annelie.

'Then why are you in such floods of tears?' asks the Moon.

'I can't help it,' says Annelie.

It's just like when Aunt Lydia was buried, she couldn't stop crying that time either.

'You'll cry yourself to death,' scolds the Moon. 'It's unhealthy. And that eerie green weed is ready and waiting for you.'

Annelie knows that the Moon is right, but she can't get her breath back between her sobs, and the sorrow is weighing down on her like the clown's apple mountain filling up the whole universe.

'Why are you crying, if I may ask?'

'Because, because, because . . .'

'Because you're sick?'

'No.'

'Because your teeth are crooked?'

'No.'

'Because you're hurting?'

'No.'

'Then why? If you won't tell me then I can't do
anything about it. What are you crying for?'

'I don't know, I don't know.'

'That's bad,' mutters the Moon. 'That's just about
the worst thing there is.'

'Where are my shoes?' says Mummy's voice.

She is speaking from the small white bedside table
with the wedding photograph on it in the silver frame.

'Mummy!' cries Annelie. 'Where have you been all
this time?'

Mummy steps out of the frame in her wedding
dress with the full skirts.

'Seeing the big wide world,' she says. She waves
her bridal bouquet and jumps down onto the floor.
'I was fed up with things. Where are my wedding
shoes?'

'They're still lying on the dyke,' says Annelie.

Mummy takes off as easily as Annelie herself and
floats over the bed.

'Open the window,' she orders.

The Moon quickly does as he is told and Mummy flies away over the houses doing perfect breastroke. Her veil and her lace skirts flutter all around her.

'Come on.' The Moon takes hold of Annelie. 'After her!'

Their course is west-south-west once again.

'She's going towards the dyke,' whispers the Moon. 'What are we to make of that?'

'She's off to Grandma's,' says Annelie. 'She's off to see Daddy.'

The Moon sighs. 'We'd best wait and see.'

Mummy alights next to the green car. For a while she stands there looking at Grandma's house and at the car. The Moon stays hanging still over the village, invisible.

'Why don't we go down and join her?'

'Sssh.'

The Moon lands behind the houses and pulls Annelie along into Grandma's house. Annelie tries to draw Mummy's attention outside by tapping on the window with a tea soldier. 'Mummy, are you coming in?'

Mummy puts the bridal bouquet down on the car and runs towards the wooden steps up the dyke.

'Where is she going?'

'Sssssh.'

Mummy disappears behind the dyke, but suddenly Annelie is able to look right through the walls of Grandma's house and through the solid thick dyke, and she sees Mummy going over to the shoes, putting them on and then walking down towards the stones in the sea. The stones aren't grey any longer but are made of glass, and the sea is no longer opaque, it is clear right down to the bottom. Mummy walks into the sea and sinks. But Snatchweed Harry's green hand plucks her out of the water and throws her back onto the land. Mummy shakes herself like a dog.

All this time Annelie has been crying as usual, for no matter what happens her sorrow won't go away. And though everything is crystal-clear now, her tears prevent her from looking at anything.

'Hush now, child.'

It's Grandma.

'Grandma, you won't go away, you won't go to

see the big wide world, will you?'

'Whatever gave you that idea? Of course I shan't.'

'Like Glum, I mean.'

'I shall always stay with you,' says Grandma.

Is it daytime? Or is it night? Are the four singers singing a song by her bedside with the Polecat giving a solo about Roses? And are those the tea soldiers marching past over the hospital floor, tapping their eighty little feet? She can hear their voices diligently marking time: 'One! Two! One! Two!' And a familiar, sharp little voice calling out in approval: 'Forward, march!'

'Go away, everybody,' thinks Annelie. She wants to sleep. Her tears are spent, she is tired.

'Aren't you going to come with us? Come on,' plead the singers, the little tea soldiers, the Mouseking and Snatchweed Harry.

But the Moon spreads his dark sail over her.

'Sssh, she's asleep.'

Yes, she's asleep. She's asleep for a hundred years, or is it a hundred hours? She is sitting on top of the dyke in the wind, in a little room made of the tall grasses all around her. She is picking flowers.

Buttercups and daisies, sorrel and clover. She sucks
on the red clover, which Grandma calls bees' bread.
And she makes a garland of buttercups and daisies,
wild pansies, which Grandma calls love-in-idleness,
and the trefoil that Grandma calls bacon-and-eggs.
There are little flat patches on the waves that never
stop moving. The light sparkles off them.

She had forgotten how lovely it is to sit and feel
the wind on the dyke when it is summer. She plaits
the garland the way Grandma has taught her, and in
her head something keeps on singing softly, and it
doesn't hurt this time, no, she likes it.

Who sings the song, and-a-one, and-a-two,
Of the little girl, and-a-one, two, three,
She lives in a kingdom by the sea so blue,
And her name is Annelie.

She lives with her Grandma, close to the dyke,
That little girl, and-a-one, two, three,
In the kingdom by the sea that the children like,
And her name is Annelie.

'Annelie? Are you awake?'

What a nice face among all these white walls and other white things. Doesn't she know that face? Tears roll like peas down to the floor. Down into the cinders?

'Are you . . . Cinderella?'

No, it isn't Cinderella.

Is it the Frock Woman?

No, it isn't the Frock Woman.

It's Mummy, isn't it?

'Are you Mummy?'

Of course it's Mummy, who else can it be!

'Are you going to stay with me?' asks Annelie sleepily.

'Yes, I'll stay with you.'

'And when I'm better? When I'm with Grandma?'

'Then I'll come every Sunday, if you want me to.'

Every Sunday. Not every day, but at least every Sunday for sure.

'Now you know,' says the Moon.

He is still dark, but there is a razor-sharp rim of light on his right-hand side, a comma of light.

'Yes, now I know.'

'Well, where shall we go?' asks the New Moon.

'To the depths of the night? To the circus? To the
sea?'

'Let's go everywhere!' cries Annelie. 'I want to go
everywhere.'

'That's the best plan,' says the New Moon. 'Far
and away the best plan. That way you'll get to know
all thirty-two points of the compass. And anyone
who knows those can never get lost.'

He blows into his sail . . .